PACK ORIGIN

A BLISSFUL OMEGAVERSE PREQUEL NOVELLA

KATE KING & JESSA WILDER

First published in 2021
King, King, Wilder, Jessa
Pack Origin: A Blissful Omegaverse Prequel Novella

Editing: One Love Editing

The Omegaverse (or A/B/O dynamics) is a speculative alternate reality where humans live in a wolf-like hierarchical social system, and take on some lycan traits such as scenting pheromones, mating for life and forming packs. People are unsure of their designation until they transition to either an alpha, beta, or omega.

The alphas tend to be larger, more athletic and more aggressive than regular humans. They have the most prominent animal instincts, and are the elite of society. Omegas are rare and physically delicate. They are the perfect biological mates to alphas, and the only ones who can have alpha or omega children. Betas are the most common designation and are essentially average humans.

There is no magic in this book. While the alphas, betas and omegas may have some animalistic instincts and practices, they are not shifters or werewolves.

PACK ORIGIN

A BLISSFUL OMEGAVERSE PREQUEL NOVELLA

INTERNATIONAL BESTSELLING AUTHORS

KATE KING JESSA WILDER

RAFE
ONE

Ares' fist slammed into the man's nose with a wet crack, and blood sprayed across the pavement, splattering on my shoes. I stepped back slightly out of the line of fire. I'd planned to help, but clearly there was no need. One punch and the beta was out cold.

My best friend and I stared at each other.

"Shit," Ares spat, echoing my thoughts. "I didn't mean to do that. Now we have to wait for him to wake up."

He let the bleeding beta drop onto the filthy ground, and I nudged the guy with the toe of my worn-out boots. I grimaced. "I don't know, man. I feel like we're going to be waiting awhile...if he wakes up at all."

Ares groaned, running one hand through his white-blond hair. The blood on his fingers turned it pinkish in the front, like some kind of boy-band idol. He frowned and wiped the rest of the blood on the inside of his leather jacket. "Dammit."

I hid half a smile. It wasn't supposed to be funny, and it

wasn't really, but if he'd paused for ten seconds to think, Ares would have realized this would happen. Betas didn't bounce back from a hit like that like an alpha would, and now we'd have to find someone else to question.

Ares bent down and rummaged in the man's pocket, unearthing a wallet, a phone, and— "Fuck, yes."

I blinked a few times, trying to focus on what he was waving in front of my face. "Car keys?"

"Yeah. How much you want to bet he left the product in his trunk?" He grinned, pale eyes flashing in the low light from the nearby streetlamp. "Come on, let's find the guys and go look for the car."

I nodded and followed Ares back through the side door into the back of the nightclub in search of our friends.

Hanging out in alleys behind clubs and beating up betas wasn't how I expected to spend my senior year of high school. Fuck, it wasn't how I expected to spend any part of my life, period. Running errands for the local gang had started as a one-off thing, but it turned out we were all pretty good at it, and the money was too good to pass up. There weren't a lot of job opportunities for teen alphas, especially foster kids. Betas tended to be afraid of us, and to be fair, that incident in the alley just now wasn't helping our case much.

My eyes darted all around the darkened club, skimming over the writhing bodies and flashing lights. This wasn't my scene at all. The smell alone was too much. The air tasted like lust, anxiety, and desperation. Like salt and burnt marshmallows.

"There." I grabbed Ares' arm and pointed across the room toward where I'd just spotted Killian and Nox cutting a path through the crowd to reach us. A head taller than everyone else, they weren't exactly blending in. Nox had his gaze fixed straight ahead while Killian was gesturing animatedly, chatting in Nox's ear as they walked.

"Find anything?" Nox asked when they reached us. His red hair had turned neon under the strobe lights, giving him the appearance of a lit match.

"Yeah, sort of," I replied, throwing Ares a sideways look.

"I'll tell you outside," Ares said, already pushing his way past a group of dancing beta girls in tight dresses to reach the exit.

The exterior of the nightclub was a standard brick warehouse, like a converted storage loft. The heavy metal door slammed behind us as we stepped out onto the darkened street and turned to face each other. The bouncer stared at us, possibly wondering if we were old enough to be here, then seemed to decide not to comment. Good choice. He smelled like a beta. Taking on four alphas wasn't a good idea, even if he was at least ten years older than us.

"What now?" Killian asked. He was practically buzzing with pent-up energy, his curly hair bouncing as he spoke.

"Parking lot," Ares replied vaguely, setting off around the side of the building and expecting that we would just follow him. Of course, we did, so he wasn't wrong.

There weren't many cars in the tiny lot. Our beat-up Impala was one of only five or six. Ares scanned the stolen key fob, then popped the trunk of a newish-looking Nissan. My eyebrows rose as we peered inside.

A dozen cardboard boxes sat stacked on top of each other. The top row was open slightly, displaying the product inside. I reached into one of the cardboard boxes and pulled out a vial, turning it over between my fingers. It smelled sickly sweet, like fruit and honey. Euphoria and lust, but manufactured.

"Fuck," Killian said, his eyes growing wide. "That's more

than I expected."

"Yeah," I agreed, not knowing what else to say.

The vials contained alpha and omega pheromones, sold to betas as party drugs. Betas couldn't usually sense things like that, but when they were concentrated like this, I guess they had some sort of temporary effect. This shipment belonged to the gang Alpha Lupi but had gotten mysteriously lost in transit when the beta that Ares knocked out in the alley decided he could take a cut for himself.

"Come on, let's take it and go. I want to do this fast and go home," Ares said harshly.

I rolled my eyes at him. No shit. We all wanted to go home and see Bliss. It didn't really need to be said.

Bliss was the only reason we did this shit anyway, and she didn't even know it.

"It's my turn," I said quietly as we strode across the grass toward the house. I hid my smile at the idea of getting to go upstairs to Bliss' room instead of ours.

Killian punched me lightly on the shoulder. "I'll trade you tonight for Saturday."

"Fuck no, 'cause on Saturday you'll forget and say it's your turn. I know how this goes."

He laughed. "Whatever, man. Worth a try."

"Quiet, both of you," Ares hissed, stopping short several paces from the front porch.

The hair on the back of my neck stood up as I listened for whatever sound had set him off. "I don't hear anything."

"Fine. Must be nothing. But be quiet—don't wake up the Wards," he snapped.

Dropping off the pheromones at the Alpha Lupi warehouse had taken longer than any of us would have liked, and we were cutting it way too close to curfew. The couple who ran our group home was already trying to get rid of us, and we didn't need to give them any more ammunition.

At the top of the stairs, the guys headed toward our room while I hovered in front of Bliss' door. Her room had a peeling plaque on it reading "Girls" in faded gold lettering. Sometimes she had up to three roommates in there, but right now, it was just her.

I slipped inside and shut the door quietly behind me, leaning against it for a moment and listening for any footsteps in the hallway.

"I heard Mr. and Mrs. Ward go to bed an hour ago," came Bliss's quiet voice.

My gaze snapped to hers. She lay on her back in the middle of her bed, staring up at the ceiling. Or rather, at the roof of the blanket tent she'd hung around her bed. She wore nothing but an oversized T-shirt and mismatched socks, and her blonde-and-purple hair fanned out across the comforter like a halo. I swallowed thickly. "Yeah? Good. We were kinda loud in the yard."

She snorted a laugh and sat up. "You think? I could hear you guys through the window. You should be more careful."

I crossed the distance between us and slipped off my shoes and T-shirt before climbing onto the bed beside her. "Yeah, I know."

"What did you do tonight, anyway?"

I ran a hand through my dark hair, unsure if I should give her any details. Ares and Nox were pretty adamant that we keep Bliss out of what we were doing with the Alpha Lupi, and I tended to agree with them. "Just work."

She huffed, rolling her eyes. "You're the worst."

I leaned over and threw an arm over her waist, tugging

her closer. "I know."

Bliss made a small, contented sigh, and my chest swelled with satisfaction. I yawned as the taste of Bliss' sleepy calm filled the air. Sleeping next to her when she was tired and projecting her feelings was like taking an extra-strength dose of melatonin, which was good, because otherwise it was almost impossible not to think about touching her. Sometimes I was glad Bliss was a beta, if only because she couldn't smell how much I wanted her.

It was beyond stupid that we kept sneaking in here to sleep next to her. Any romantic relationships between foster siblings were grounds for instant relocation. We were risking way too much for this. But Bliss had nightmares, and none of us could stand to smell her terror from down the hall night after night, so the risk was worth it.

"I had an idea today," she muttered into my arm.

"What?"

"I feel like when we age out of the system, we should move to California."

I barked a laugh. "Why? You've never been there."

"I don't know. I saw some propaganda thing on TV for the Omega Institute today, and that's out in California, and it just made me think it sounds warm out there. I just want to go somewhere warm."

"Sure. Warm sounds good."

She yawned and nodded, snuggling deeper under her blanket. I pulled her closer into my shoulder and made a mental note to mention this to the guys tomorrow. With all the money we were making running errands for the gang, we probably could move out to California. Or wherever.

In reality, we'd always find a way to do whatever she needed. Because every single one of us was in love with her, and every decision started and ended with Bliss.

BLISS
TWO

Bliss: Where did you guys go last night?

My nose scrunched up as three bubbles appeared and disappeared in the group text. It was like they made a pact to keep me out of the loop.

“Bliss, can you head down to Mrs. Clark’s office after class?”

I looked up from where I’d been hiding my phone under my desk and made slightly guilty eye contact with my English teacher, Mr. Williams, across the room. *Crap.* I stuffed the phone in between my knees. “Why?”

He gave me a look that told me in no uncertain terms he’d seen me texting but just sighed and waved a slip of yellow paper at me. “It doesn’t say. The note just asks that you head down there ASAP.”

“But I have algebra,” I said feebly. You knew it was bad if I’d rather go to algebra.

Mr. Williams just shrugged and turned back to the smart board, effectively dismissing me. I sighed. *Please kill me.*

I'd been called down to see Mrs. Clark, the ancient and holier-than-thou high school guidance counselor, at least once a month ever since my freshman year. At first I thought it was just because I was a foster kid, but there were a bunch of kids from the group home at my school, and none of them ever had to go see Mrs. Clark. Apparently, I was just lucky. Or cursed. Whatever.

My phone buzzed again, and I subtly checked it between my knees.

Killian: Miss me?

Rafe: She just saw you, Asshole.

When the bell rang, I got up, swung my backpack over my shoulder, straightened my sundress, and headed for the door. No one paid me much attention as I went. No one ever really did—except for Mrs. Clark, obviously.

"Hi, Sandra." I threw a smile at the school secretary as I entered the office.

Sandra looked up from her computer and blinked a couple of times at me. Her blonde whisper bangs fluttered as she spoke, brushing the top of her cat-eye glasses. "Hello again, Bliss. What can I do for you this time?"

I struggled not to roll my eyes. "I don't know. Mrs. Clark wanted to see me?"

She laughed lightly. "Oh. I thought it might be about those boys again."

I shook my head. In fairness to Sandra, the other reason I was often in the school office usually had to do with my four best friends. They weren't the best at staying out of trouble.

"You can wait there, dear." Sandra pointed to a black plastic chair.

I sat down, dropping my backpack and pulling out my

phone again. Of course, in the last ten minutes, it had exploded with unanswered messages in the group chat.

Killian: Bonfire at the spot tonight.

Nox: K.

Ares: I have to work.

Killian: Come after.

Rafe: I'll get the booze.

Killian: B, what do you think?

Nox: Bliss, where are you?

Ares: What the hell does that mean?

Nox: She's not in algebra.

Rafe: What the fuck?

Me: I just got called into guidance. Please try not to hulk out.

The door to the guidance office opened, and I whipped my head up, instinctively flipping my phone facedown on my bare thigh.

Mrs. Clark stood in the doorway wearing a navy blue suit, her graying hair pulled into a tight ponytail. She smiled. "Sorry, Bliss. I didn't mean to startle you."

"You didn't."

"Why don't you come on in."

The office was tiny and drab, just like the rest of the school. Everything in our town had needed updating since 1985, but there wasn't any government funding to do it. As much as I didn't like Mrs. Clark, you had to respect being a high school guidance counselor in such a dismal town.

She gestured for me to take a seat in the chair in front of her desk and sat down across from me. She folded her hands and gave me a smile reminiscent of visiting a sick relative in the hospital. "How are you doing?"

"Um, fine."

"I like your hair. It's so original."

I almost laughed as my hand flew involuntarily to where I'd dyed the bottom few inches of my pale blonde hair neon purple. Her comment had a very "hello, fellow kids" vibe. "Thanks."

I tensed, knowing that whatever bizarre thing she wanted to talk to me about was right around the corner. My grades, my life at the group home, my relationship with my friends, all seemed to be fair game. Lucky me.

"So, I called you in today because I wanted to chat about what you plan to do after high school."

I blinked at her. That was at least a somewhat normal subject for a guidance counselor to bring up—unlike a month ago when she went on a weirdly obsessive rant about my friends. Still, she'd unintentionally touched on a sore subject. I was turning seventeen soon, which meant I only had a year left until I aged out of the foster care system. All my friends had already turned seventeen, so we were quickly running out of time to make money and a plan. Actually, maybe Mrs. Clark *did* know that.

"This is the time when you should apply to colleges," Mrs. Clark said. She clearly hadn't noticed my moment of reflection.

I snorted. "Ma'am, I'm sorry, but college requires money. There is no chance I can afford to go anywhere."

She smiled and pushed a stack of papers toward me. "There are lots of government grants and scholarships for betas. I know it might sometimes seem like only alphas get that kind of leg up in education, but you just need to know where to look."

I glanced down at the top brochure and frowned. It was for a betas' college in the Midwest. Well, that wasn't going to work. "Er, thanks. I'll think about it," I lied.

Mrs. Clark gave me a shrewd look. Maybe she was used

to kids lying to her, or maybe she just knew me well enough by now, but I got the strong feeling she didn't believe me. "Bliss, can I offer you some advice?"

No. "Sure."

"You need to start putting your own best interests first and thinking realistically about your situation."

I blinked at her, my fingers knotting in the fabric of my skirt. "What does that mean?"

Her eyes darted to the side, like she was choosing her words carefully. "If I'm being frank, with no family and no plan, you don't have a lot of good prospects."

"I have a family," I said automatically, indignation rising in my stomach.

"Your...friends aren't going to provide a stable future for you. Packs don't form around betas."

"Um, I mean..."

"Those boys you hang around with are still young, but alphas get possessive. You could end up hurt."

My heart pounded in my ears. I'd heard this kind of thing before from my foster parents, teachers, random girls at school. People just didn't get it. They didn't understand *us.* "Ma'am, I don't know what you think is going on, but we're just friends." I forced myself to maintain a neutral expression. "We can't have any relationships like that at the group home. Nothing is going on."

She gave me a "yeah, right" look. I wished I could tell her that, unfortunately, the second part of that was completely true. "Bliss..."

"Thanks for your advice. Was that it? I think the bell's about to ring."

She stood as well, smoothing her hair. "Yes, but please take the college brochure."

"Uh-huh." I grabbed one at random and stuffed it in my bag.

Mrs. Clark walked around her desk and swung the door open for me and then halted in her tracks. I peeked over her shoulder, and my face split into a grin.

Thank God.

The chair where I'd waited was now occupied once more, this time by one of my best friends. Killian's head popped up when the door opened, his chestnut curls bouncing, and he stood up to his full—considerable—height.

Behind him, Rafe leaned against the wall, seeming to want to blend into the shadows with his dark hair, black eyes, and all-black clothing. His tan and sharp jaw made him look like the star of some teen drama, and he absolutely knew it. He grinned at me over Mrs. Clark's shoulder, and my heart beat faster.

"Hey, B," Killian said loudly, trying to reach for me.

Mrs. Clark visibly stiffened. She, like most betas, was probably afraid of all alphas, even if they were seventeen. I didn't really blame her. Except for my guys, most alphas scared me too. Their size and strength were enough, but add in their ability to control a room with just their bark, and I saw no reason to mess with them.

"All set?" Killian asked, half to me and half to our guidance counselor.

Mrs. Clark paused, and for a minute, I thought she was going to shove me back in the office and slam the door, but then she relented. "Yes. Bliss, you can go."

Killian grinned. His height and muscle mass made him look old for his age, but his cheeks were still slightly rounded with youth, and his damn dimples made him more adorable than hardened. Even if he didn't look at least five years older than seventeen.

Rafe pushed off the wall to stand on my other side as we left the office. "What the hell was that about?"

I had to tilt my head all the way back to look up at him. It was the same with all four of the guys. It had been clear from the time they were children they would turn out to be alphas, but in the last couple of years, things had really gotten out of control in the size department. It was like I woke up and suddenly all my friends were a foot taller than me and sporting muscles on their muscles. I was still waiting to morph into the standard willowy tall beta, like I remembered my mother being. In the meantime, I'd seemed to have stalled out at 5'2".

"Nothing important," I said truthfully. I definitely would not be dwelling on that conversation if I could help it.

Killian's eyes were skeptical, but he didn't push it. "Come on, we're skipping out on last period."

I laughed as he grabbed my hand and pulled me toward the double doors to the school parking lot.

"Why?"

Killian winked. "Because we can."

I stood in the shadows of an overflowing dumpster in a darkened alley, my back up against the brick wall of a shabby convenience store. The low, flickering streetlamp cast the only light, and the dumpster was giving off the distinct smell of week-old food. I could honestly say I would have preferred to go to algebra than hang out here.

I took a few steps to the left to distance myself from the

dumpster, the filthy water from a puddle splashing against the hem of my sundress. My heart sank. *Gross.*

Beside me, Killian laughed. "Don't tell me you're prissy all of a sudden?"

"There's 'prissy,' and then there's 'oh my God that smells disgusting.' Don't judge."

I slapped the back of my hand against his entirely too firm stomach and glared up at him. He made a satisfying oomph sound, making me smirk, even if he was faking it for my benefit.

"Come on, B. You don't gotta play that way." His homey scent overpowered me, blocking out the reeking garbage as he wrapped one of his heavy arms around me in a bear hug, lifting me off the ground away from the puddle.

I squirmed against the familiar hold, pinching his side as laughter bubbled its way out of my mouth. "Let go of me!"

"Make me." His threat was completely undermined by the laugh in his voice and the way he stood primed to attack me.

"Betas have skills too, you know," I said between gasps of laughter. His smirk took up his entire face. "Yeah? Show me."

"Listen—"

Blue and red lights reflected off the side of the building, cutting me off. Killian hauled me behind the dumpster and out of view of the street just in time for the cop car to pass. I let out a breath.

We weren't doing anything wrong...at least, not yet. Rafe was the one in the store getting the alcohol, and he wasn't back. It wasn't like the cops could give Killian and me a ticket for loitering. What they would do, though, was run our names and drag us back to the group home. The last time we got caught, our punishment was a weekend in isolation. A shiver ran through me at the thought.

Killian ran his hand up and down my arm as the lights from the cop car disappeared. He grinned down at me and shook his honey-brown hair out of his deep brown eyes, only for it to flop back in place, skimming the tops of sharp cheekbones.

"You need a haircut."

He glanced down at my hair, eyes maybe lingering for half a second longer than usual on where the ends brushed my chest in my thin dress. "Nah, never. If I need a haircut, so do you."

"Shut your mouth." I grinned, fingering the ends of my mostly blonde hair.

Killian's eyes were slow to meet mine. "I like the purple."

"Got it." Rafe jogged up the dark street, interrupting our conversation, a wicked smile across his mouth. In his all-black attire, he blended in with the night.

"Hurry up," I hissed, reaching out for the bag in his hand as I looked around.

"Chill, we're good." He handed the brown paper bag to me with a grin.

I shoved the vodka, bag and all, into my backpack. "Come on, let's go."

I wasn't being dramatic—at least, I didn't think so. There weren't any second chances at the group home, and underage drinking was definitely on the list of offenses that would get you kicked out. Fast. My gaze bounced around, looking for anything that might get us caught. The faster we got out of here, the better.

Rafe glanced down at me, taking in my rigid posture, and slipped his fingers below my jaw. "Relax. We've got this."

I frowned. I hated when the guys downplayed things. "Mmmhmm."

Rafe's skeptical gaze scanned my face, and he rubbed his thumb over the seam of my pinched brows. His voice dipped low. "There's nothing to worry about, Bliss. No one's getting caught."

I entwined my fingers with his, swinging our arms as we walked. "Whatever. The guys are waiting."

The park was only a few blocks up the road, and I followed Killian through the winding path surrounded by trees, Rafe close behind us. The crisp night air nipped at my hair and ears, and I was grateful to see the light from the fire up ahead. Either Nox or Ares—hopefully both—were already here.

Our spot wasn't anything special. A small clearing in the center of a grove of secluded trees. The previous summer, we'd built a fire pit and scrounged up a collection of old lawn chairs, logs, and one moth-eaten old couch to furnish our home away from home. It still wasn't great, but anything was better than the group home.

My footsteps crunched over twigs and dead leaves as we approached, announcing our arrival. Nox lay stretched out on the ratty couch, like he had sprinted all the way from school just to get the best spot first. Honestly, he probably did. He glanced up as we came into view, his slightly freckled face splitting into a grin. "Hey!"

Killian flopped down on a lawn chair on the far side, a smile taking over his face. "Hey, brother."

I rolled my eyes at the theatrics as I dropped my schoolbag and sat on the arm of the sofa. I reached for the book Nox had discarded when we arrived. "What are you reading?"

"Nothing you would like."

"You don't know that." I grinned, even as I tried to look offended.

"Uh, yeah I do, but be my guest if you want to bore yourself to tears."

I raked my fingers absently through the tips of his copper-brown hair while flipping through the book with the other. "Yeah, I don't know about this." I pretended to grimace. "I'm going to leave the extra-credit English assignments to you."

He leaned into my touch like a cat, and a soft rumbling sound came from his chest. I snatched my hand away. Nox's arm wrapped around my middle and dragged me over his lap to sit beside him. He kept my legs draped over his, and I rested my head in the crook of his arm to hide my flaming face.

"It's fine, Bliss, I'm a guy. Cut me some slack."

"Mmmhmm."

That was the problem though. Lately I didn't want to cut them slack--any of them. The last year had been filled with barely there touches and not so accidental grazes, but nothing ever came of it, and it couldn't. At least, not right now.

"Where's Ares?" My gaze flicked around the clearing as if he'd suddenly appear.

Rafe stood by the fire and tossed a few hot dogs on the grate over the fire. "He's working, remember?"

"Oh, yeah." A sick feeling flipped my stomach. Lately, it seemed like one of them was always missing. They'd been showing up with money, and I knew for a fact they hadn't picked up any legitimate jobs. "I supposed you're not going to tell me where he went though?"

Nox squeezed my knee, and Rafe gave me an apologetic shrug. "No idea, actually. Sorry."

"Whatever..." I mumbled under my breath.

"I'm here." Ares' thick voice met my ears before his face became visible from the path. His pale blue eyes and white-blond hair would have made him look almost angelic if his smirk wasn't so self-satisfied. Clearly, he'd heard me. "Alright, Love?"

Relief washed through me at the sight of him, quickly followed by a tinge of anger as he slid an envelope stamped with a crescent moon—the symbol of the local gang—into the pocket of his leather jacket. I ground my teeth. "Yup."

Ares took the seat next to Killian and pulled a Sharpie out of his pocket to doodle something on his calf. "What did I miss?"

"Nothing," I said honestly.

He looked up at me, eyes almost fluorescent in the flickering light. "Why were you in guidance again?"

"Oh..." The back of my neck heated. I didn't even know why I was embarrassed; it was so damn stupid. I chuckled awkwardly, trying to make it no big deal. "Just another person sticking their nose where it doesn't need to be."

"Meaning what?" Rafe's tone was just on the edge of turning dangerous.

Killian stood up and cleared his throat, drawing my attention to him. "Scoot over." He plopped down on Nox's left, pulling my legs into his lap and running his fingers over my calves.

"Bliss, what happened with guidance?" Rafe asked again impatiently, sitting on Killian's now empty chair.

I tilted my head, searching Rafe's face across the fire. His hooded gaze branded me, making my skin heat. I licked my dry lips. He never looked at me like that...at least, not that I'd noticed. "It's not a big deal," I said, looking down. "Just wanted to remind me packs don't form around betas. We're different, so it's not worth talking about."

Ares growled, and my eyes flashed to him, as though I'd been summoned...or something. His eyes went dark, and I had a sudden, almost uncontrollable urge to stand and go over there. The air tasted different, like iron and wool.

"C'mere, Little Wolf." Nox reached for me again and picked me up easily, placing me on his lap. My back tucked in against his chest, and his chin rested on my shoulder. "Ignore her. They just don't get it."

I nodded. That was true. Our situation wasn't normal, but then again, nothing about our lives had ever been normal.

Our group home was state run, specializing in placements for teen alphas. It was hard to find permanent foster care for them because people considered them aggressive, especially after years in the system. That wasn't exactly untrue, but it was still shitty and unfair. My guys had all bounced in and out of foster care as kids, but because they all came from an alpha parent and it was clear where things were headed, none of them had ever been adopted.

I'd ended up in the group home by chance. My beta mother had dropped me off when I was five and never came back. I'd been fostered out several times but kept getting sent back to the group home. As a beta, it should've been easy for me to find a permanent home, but it never was. The longer I was away from my guys, the more miserable I became. It was a deep ache that grew each day we were apart, and no amount of pretending could hide it forever. All the foster parents eventually sent me back, trading me in like a used car for a younger, happier model.

Every time I came back, my guys were waiting for me. My family. My pack. The thought of being permanently separated from them made my heart twist in my chest. Not after all of these years and everything we'd been through. They wiped my tears when I scraped my knees, beat up school bullies, and loved me when no one else would.

We were family, and family took care of each other.

Rafe's attention focused on me, his elbows on his knees, where he sat across the fire from us beside Ares. His shoulders were stiff, and my gaze settled on a muscle that ticked in his jaw. Energy snapped between us, sizzling in the air, but he leaned back, breaking the moment. The light of the fire cast shadows over his face until all I could see was his piercing gaze. "Next week's your seventeenth birthday."

I leapt on the change of topic like a starving animal on an all-you-can-eat buffet. "We all know that's not my real birthday," I said too fast, playing it off like it didn't matter, but a twinge of pain stung my chest. My mom didn't bother to leave a birth certificate when she dropped me on the center's doorstep. The best they got out of her was I was five, and she was clearly a beta. Knowing your designation was a main staple of our lives, so at least I knew that.

Ares gave me an intense stare, and when he spoke, his voice was low and assertive. "It counts to the system, which just means we only have a year left to figure out where we're going."

"Five months." I grinned. "You're almost eighteen."

He nodded, conceding the point.

"You two are so serious." Killian leaned over the edge of the couch to grab my abandoned backpack and pull out the vodka. "We should be talking about a birthday party, not this stressful shit."

I smiled at him, holding out a hand. "Give me some of that, then."

He took a deep swig before handing it to me. The cheap

liquid burned my throat, forcing me to clear it, but it warmed my stomach when it settled.

Nox did the same, then screwed the lid on and tossed it to the guys across from us. The mix of heat from the liquor pooling in my stomach and Nox pressed against my back left my body languid. I needed to get off him before I did something stupid. "Kill, move over. I need room."

He shifted until there was enough space for me to slip between them, but he grumbled something about being comfortable while doing it.

I made a high-pitched noise when they both pressed into me. Warm energy coursed through my center, and Nox's hand clamped around my thigh, holding me still. I slammed my mouth shut—*oh my God, what the hell was that?*

Killian moved closer so that his leg lined up against Nox's, but neither of them mentioned it. Sweat trickled down my neck, and I lifted my hair to expose it to the cool air. Was it hot out here? Did we really need that many logs on the fire? Except when I looked at the fire, the embers were nearly out.

Nox's soft growl rumbled against my side as his nose traced a line of my neck. "You smell good, Bliss. Almost like...I'm not sure. But I like it."

I focused on the others, and they all stared back at me with that same hungry expression. The taste of smoke and honey hit my tongue, as though it was filling the air, and my mouth started to water.

"Knock it off," I croaked out.

"Truth or dare, Bliss?" Killian asked, and an unexpected spicy taste of mischief filled my mouth. I expected the guys to protest, make a big deal about such a childish game, but they were all leaning toward me, waiting for my answer.

I swallowed hard, and a trickle of excitement ran down

my spine as the full weight of their attention sank in. "Okay, fine, but I'm not going first. Someone else go."

"I'll go first. Dare," Rafe said, looking directly at me, and waited for my question.

Too nervous to ask anything I actually wanted, I bit my lip and asked, "Jump the fire."

His brow raised, his eyes rolling, and he made quick work of it. "You're going to have to think of better dares than that."

I squirmed in my seat. The distinctive feel of his alpha bark ran up my spine. "No fair. No coercion."

He just smiled and shrugged.

Ass.

No one picked truth. Instead, each dare became increasingly riskier as the night went on and the vodka made its rounds. When Killian stripped down naked and ran through the woods, I damn near swallowed my tongue. When he got back, he took his time redressing, and I soaked up every detail, unable to look away. His chest was cut with muscles, each one forming a hill and valley. My mouth watered as his muscles flexed, and his skin pebbled under my gaze. My eyes drifted lower just in time to make out the shape of his knot before his shorts covered him. I snapped to his dark, hooded eyes, and a slow smirk formed on his lips.

The taste of honey filled my mouth again. We'd never passed this line. It was practically a cardinal in to admit that anything more developed between all of us. I knew all too well how fast the system would move you if you were caught in a relationship with another member. We couldn't risk losing each other.

Ares held my stare, ice-blue eyes mesmerizing in the dying light of the flames. "Your turn, Love."

I swallowed hard. Nerves had my stomach fluttering. "Dare."

His jaw twitched, and his eyes darted around to his friends before returning to me. He bit his bottom lip with too-sharp teeth, expression turning wicked. "Kiss Rafe."

I sucked in a sharp breath. That was crossing the line, and we all knew it. I avoided Rafe's gaze, instead watching the other three guys for their reactions. Their eyes were hooded, and no one disagreed.

I stood from the couch and wavered on my feet. Nox reached out to steady me, his fingers practically spanning my entire waist. My heart beat out a pounding rhythm as I slowly circled the fire. I stilled, frozen in place directly in front of Rafe. His gaze was like a brand across my skin, and heat flooded through my chest. I wet my lips, and his eyes zeroed in on the movement.

When I didn't budge, he stood up and stepped closer until there was barely an inch between us. His head dipped down, black eyes searched mine, and his tongue wet his bottom lip. Heat flooded me. I wanted this. I'd wanted this for a while now.

His mouth brushed featherlight against mine. The barely there touch set me off like a Roman candle, and I stole the inches between us, opening my mouth against his, practically begging him to take it. He didn't disappoint, sliding his tongue against mine, pulling a moan from my throat. My fingers tightened on his shirt, holding him in place, then pushing him away. A liquid fiery feeling filled my limbs, and a buzz inside me begged to press harder against him. A faint scent of jasmine wrapped around me, and four deep growls filled the air.

Rafe ripped away from me, and a pained whimper escaped my lips before I could stop it. I didn't want the kiss to end. My body practically ached to continue. Rafe's hands slid across my jaw, cupping my face, and his fingers trembled as he held me. His gaze glued to me, eyes flipping back and forth between mine before he shook his head and stepped back.

I stood there, frozen, my entire body shaking. Something had shifted in the air, something big.

A tinge of worry pinched at my chest, but that was stupid. I was their beta. This was the natural progression. Just not yet.

I walked back to my spot on the couch. Neither Nox nor Killian touched me, no more hand holding or slow circles on my arm. Rafe kept his eyes on his shoes, while Ares studied me, his brows pinched together and his mouth tight.

What the hell did we just do?

NOX
THREE

Killian grunted as he pushed a textbook off the edge of my bed. "I don't know how you even sleep in all this."

I ignored the uneven spines of the books digging into my back. "You can always sit on your own bed."

"Nah, you wouldn't want that." Killian dropped his feet to the hardwood floor and sat up, the muscles in his back tensing under his thin, white T-shirt. He smirked. "Everyone knows I'm the only one who'll get in it with you."

I rolled my eyes. *Fuck, he's annoying.*

I jammed my foot against his back, trying to push him off, but only succeeded in knocking a few more books to the floor. I really did need a shelf. "Oh, right. 'Cause you're with a different girl every night? Can't wait to explain that to Bliss."

Killian's honey-brown eyes drained of all playfulness. "Don't even start, man. It's been over a year, and you know it."

"Yeah, okay," I said, a sarcastic edge to my voice.

His hand whipped out, grabbing the neck of my shirt, and I laughed, twisting as I tried to break his hold on me. He was way too defensive about this. We'd all messed around, but Kill was always crawling with girls. He was right though —in the last year, he had put an end to it.

"Cut that shit out." Ares' low command pierced through me. I had half a mind to ignore him just to prove I could, but ignoring a bark took effort, and this wasn't important.

Killian dropped my shirt immediately and looked toward where Ares sat on his bed directly beside mine.

Never able to resist a smart-ass comment, Killian turned his smirk toward Ares. "Oh sorry, didn't realize you'd become a monk. Hypocrite."

Ares raised one eyebrow at Kill across the room. "You have no idea what I do. Bliss does, so shut the fuck up."

I frowned. I wasn't totally sure what that meant, but he was right. We didn't know. Unlike Killian, Ares liked to keep his rotation hidden.

About a year ago, we all started noticing Bliss making excuses to leave every time a girl was around us. Which was often. At first, we were just less obvious about our hookups, but even the idea we were hurting her had us all stopping completely. It didn't take a genius to know we were all just filling space, waiting for her.

I rubbed my palms over my eyes. It had been a long-ass night.

Rafe strode through the room and sat next to Ares. His dark hair stuck up in all directions like he'd been running his hand through it. He'd immediately taken off when we got back to the group home.

"Nice of you to show up," Ares said sardonically.

"Yeah, well, I needed to think."

"I dared her to *kiss* you." Ares punched him in the arm. Hard. "You weren't supposed to *maul* her."

Rafe grunted and narrowed his eyes at Ares. "Don't you think I know that?" He dropped his head in his hands like he needed the extra support. "I couldn't help it."

I leaned forward, setting my jaw. "Couldn't or wouldn't?"

His eyes met mine. "You think you could have her on you like that and not react?"

I looked at the ceiling and adjusted myself in my pants, trying not to picture the whole thing. "Why would you dare them to do that?" I asked Ares incredulously. "There was no world where that was going to go well."

He shrugged. "I don't know. I was drunk, and I didn't think they'd actually do it."

Lie. We could all taste the lie the moment he spoke. With our metabolism, he'd have to drink an entire handle of vodka to get drunk, and he absolutely knew Rafe would jump at the chance to kiss Bliss. Any of us would.

"Bullshit." I glared at him. "At least try to lie better."

He rolled his eyes. "No, I'm good."

"So, what is it? You're trying to push us into breaking the rules early? Well, stop. All we have to do is be patient for one more year until we get out of this shithole."

Ares' icy-blue gaze bored into mine. His voice was low and serious, as if he was proposing a bank robbery instead of dating our girl. Might as well have been. "What if we lay it out for Bliss? Just tell her now and see what happens."

Rafe's head jerked up to Ares. "Woah, wait. We haven't told her because we know damn well none of us are turning her down if she gives us the green light."

Killian's chest rumbled beside me, stealing all of our attention. "I'm in. That's exactly what I want. Fuck the plan."

I clenched my teeth, fighting back the pull to agree with

him. Usually if we disagreed on anything between the four of us, it was Ares and Rafe versus me and Killian, but right now, things were split all wrong.

It was never a question of whether we wanted it. I'd kill to have her now, but I wasn't stupid enough to risk everything. I stood from the bed and pinned each one of them with a glare. "The Wards are already watching us like hawks. They'll separate us if they find a shred of proof something's going on. That sound better to you?"

I walked out of our room, my skin practically crawling with anxiety. I should leave and cool the hell off, but I couldn't ignore the magnetic pull coming from Bliss' room. No one calmed me like she did. It wasn't my turn to sleep with her tonight, but I didn't care. Whoever's turn it was was going to need to share or swap.

The girls' room was smaller than ours. They didn't stay here long. Not in a place designed for soon-to-be alphas. Instead, they used it as almost a rest stop between homes.

All except Bliss.

The way Rafe had devoured her, drawing out shallow, edible noises, made me burn with the need to press myself into them. The entire world narrowed, darkening at the edges until it was just them. It felt like years had culminated for that moment, everyone forgetting exactly why we'd never crossed that line.

We all wanted her. And we all *knew* we wanted her. She was the only one too blind to see it. But there was something different tonight. Something more.

The second their mouths parted, the overwhelming feeling that everything had changed washed over me. The realization of how far he'd gone left the air frozen. Like pressing pause on a movie right before the finale.

I slid the door closed behind me, halting momentarily

when it whined. I didn't want to have to explain why I was sneaking into Bliss' room in the middle of the night. No doors opened. They never did.

The room was empty of her presence, but the window on the far wall was lifted a few inches from the sill. Cold air drifted through it.

I climbed through the window after her, my shoulders scraping the frame and the sleeves of my hoodie catching on the sides. This used to be an easy fit. The rough grit of the shingles kept my footing sure as I made my way around the side and lifted myself onto the barely angled roof. My breath came out on a sigh at the sight of Bliss' silhouette illuminated by the streetlight. Her knees were tucked to her chest, and she curled over them to rest her chin on top.

Her head jerked up at the sound of my footsteps making their way toward her. Her blonde hair was pulled into a high ponytail, the purple tips impossible to make out in the low light.

"I thought you'd be here."

Her lips tipped up in a tentative smile, and she stretched her legs out in front of her. "You've always been the first to find me."

I lowered myself down beside her, close enough to feel her pressed against my side. The chill of her pajama pants seeped into my thigh. Her arms were covered in goosebumps, and she vibrated with a slight tremble. Fuck, she was freezing.

I pulled my hoodie off with one hand and pulled it over her head. My chest rumbled silently, pleased at the sight of her engulfed in my clothes, and wrapped my arm around her.

"How long have you been up here?" I asked, tucking her shivering body closer to my side.

She shrugged against me. "Not long."

Liar.

Bliss came up here whenever she was thinking too hard, letting worry take over. She thought she needed space from us, but her shoulders relaxed every time we found her, as if she'd been waiting for me the entire time.

I took a deep breath, debating on calling her on her bullshit. Instead, I laid us both flat and tucked her against my chest, staring up at the stars like we'd done a thousand nights before.

I pointed at a formation of three stars. "Orion's belt."

She vibrated against me with her laugh. "You always find that one. You'd think you'd start somewhere more creative."

We'd done this so often I could pick out any constellation, but I liked the way it made her laugh each time I pointed at the protective hunter.

She pointed out constellation after constellation. The normalcy had her relaxing into me. "What's that one's story?"

I laughed. Of course she'd choose that one. I adjusted the story slightly each time I told it. "The bear. Zeus turned his girlfriend into a bear in order to protect her and hide any sign they'd been together." My skin itched, and my chest tightened as I went on. "One day when he left her, a hunter made a killing shot. When Zeus found her dead, still in bear form, he sent her to the stars to remember her forever."

She shuddered against me. "I don't like that one."

"You don't like any of them. The Greeks told miserable stories."

She snuggled deeper into my sweater and took deep breaths. Each one had her eyes drooping further.

I kept my voice low, resting my head on hers. "Why are you out here?"

She stiffened in my arms, but I didn't let her pull away. Moments passed before she answered. "I don't want anything to change."

It was my turn to stiffen. The idea that she wanted to stay friends forever didn't sit well with me, and I knew it wouldn't sit well with the guys. I pushed out my next words, knowing the guys would kill me if I screwed this up. "I think you know things are changing. You felt it, same as us."

My heart slammed into my chest with each second it took her to respond.

She tilted her head until she met my gaze. "They could separate us."

I grabbed her chin and stared down with every ounce of surety I felt. "Never."

The following morning, I woke to sunlight streaming through the gauzy material of the canopy I'd hung around my bed. The sun warmed my skin—hotter than it should have been. Nox and Ares' scent still clung to the sheets, and I snuggled my nose in deeper. They were gone, of course, always up and out of my room before the house woke up.

I took one last inhale before lifting my head and swiping hair out of my face. Warmth heated my body from the inside out, like I was running a fever. Or I'd been having a nightmare I'd somehow already forgotten.

Maybe I drank more than I realized last night.

I swung my legs over the side of my bed and put my bare feet on the cold, dusty floor. There were no other girls in my age group staying at the house right now, so I had my room to myself for a couple of weeks—small mercies.

Sounds already emanated from every corner of the house, despite the early hour. I could hear Rafe and Killian talking over the sound of the radio down the hall, and pots and pans banged downstairs where Mrs. Ward was no doubt cooking breakfast for some of the younger kids. That was the thing about living in a group home—no matter how hard you tried, there was no sleeping in.

At least everything seemed normal.

Images of last night came flooding back to me, and my skin seemed to heat another few degrees. That hadn't been my first kiss by any means. I wasn't even a virgin, thanks to one jealousy-induced fling I had last summer, but this was my first time kissing any of my guys. Some invisible line seemed was crossed, and I was simultaneously thrilled and terrified.

It was April, but still, for whatever reason, the weather hadn't quite decided if it was winter or spring yet. I compromised by throwing an oversized sweatshirt over cutoff shorts and slipping my feet into Converse sneakers. The blue hooded sweatshirt had either belonged to Rafe or Nox originally. I couldn't remember anymore. It was so long it covered my shorts like a dress. The fabric stuck to my flaming skin, and I strode over to the tiny mirror in the corner. I looked okay. Maybe a little better than okay—kind of...glowy, actually.

I pulled my hair over my shoulder to get it off my neck and fanned myself with the back of my hand. There was literally no chance that Mr. and Mrs. Ward would let me stay home from school even if I was running a fever, so I needed to suck it up. I opened the door to my room and took the stairs two at a time, thinking maybe the fresh air outside would help. If the guys weren't already out by the car, I'd wait for them on the porch.

Our house was shabby but relatively large. Big enough to house up to twelve foster kids at a time, at least. Right now, we had eight—the four guys, me, and three younger kids all under the age of ten. The little kids never lasted long here, especially if they didn't look like they were going to grow up to be alphas. This group would all get sent to more permanent placement within the week. It sucked—I loved playing with the kids while they were here. It was hard not to get attached.

At the bottom of the stairs, I grabbed my backpack off the coat rack and practically sprinted out the front door.

"Bliss."

I froze in my tracks. *Shit.* Doubling back a few steps, I turned slowly. "Hey, Mr. Ward. Sorry, I didn't see you."

Mr. Ward, one half of the couple who ran our group home, sat at the kitchen counter reading the newspaper. An alpha in his late fifties, he had graying hair and lines around his eyes but otherwise looked good for his age, and he liked to make sure everyone knew it. Not that that was unusual for an alpha, but he made it seem like he was the second coming.

He lowered his paper slowly and deliberately ran his gaze up and down my body. He was already dressed for work, wearing his police uniform. My skin crawled as his eyes lingered too long on my legs and then traveled up to my chest. He took a deep breath through his nose, his eyes narrowing. "Are you heading to school?"

"Yup," I said, trying to keep my voice light. "It's Friday."

He took another deep breath, gazing at me. He was always staring at me when his wife and the guys weren't around. "You were out late last night."

"Not past curfew," I blurted. "I had to work."

"Uh-huh." He nodded and tapped his spoon on the edge of his coffee mug.

I took a step toward the door. *Okay—that wasn't too bad.*

"Wait, Bliss," he called, a bark in his voice.

I froze. *Goddamnit.*

I turned, the compulsion to obey almost impossible to ignore. "Yes?"

"How are your grades?"

"Uh, fine." I danced from foot to foot, my eyes darting around the kitchen. I needed to sit down or something. I could actually feel my skin getting warmer, though now it was accompanied by nervous nausea.

"Good. Don't want you getting distracted by those gang-bangers."

Anger curled in my stomach. "That's not—"

His muscles rippled under his sweater, and it made the back of my neck crawl. I broke off. Most alphas—my guys excluded—scared me. Mr. Ward had never touched me, but I always felt like there was a "yet" at the end of that sentence. *I need to get out of here.*

The stairs creaked behind me, and both Mr. Ward and I glanced up. Ares leaned against the wall at the bottom of the stairs, black backpack slung over one shoulder, wearing a tight black T-shirt that showed off the tattoos that he'd started accumulating on his heavily muscled arms. His white-blond hair was a little long on the top and fell into bored, icy eyes.

My heart beat against my ribs, and my stomach leapt in some strange mixture of anxiety and excitement. Ares' nostrils flared, and his eyes flashed to me for half a second before darting back toward Mr. Ward. "You good, Bliss?"

I nodded slowly. It was almost weird when he used my real name—though, of course, any nicknames in front of the Wards would be a terrible idea.

"Shouldn't you be at school?" Mr. Ward sneered.

"Yeah. We both should." Ares took a protective step toward me, and Mr. Ward's eyes flashed.

As a beta, I couldn't smell pheromones—not the way alphas and omegas could—but I could swear, even I noticed something going on here. As Ares and Mr. Ward stared each other down, the level of testosterone in the room quadrupled, I was sure of it.

I took a step further back toward Ares and grabbed him by the wrist, pulling his gaze to mine. For half a second, his eyes turned dark as he looked down at me. "Let's go. We're going to be late," I said pointedly.

To my surprise, he let me pull him out onto the porch and down to the driveway, where the other three guys waited by the car. Mr. Ward's eyes bored holes into the back of my neck as we left. I glanced back, and sure enough, he stood at the window, his gaze fixed on where I was still clutching Ares' wrist. Damnit. I dropped his hand quickly, but it made no difference as he slung an arm over my shoulders instead. I sighed, torn between telling him to back off for the sake of appearances and liking his warm scent.

"Finally," Nox called across the yard as we approached, waving at us. In the sun, his hair and scruffy stubble was particularly ginger, as opposed to their usual red brown. "I have Mr. Roberts first period, and he's always up my ass for being late."

I gave him an apologetic shrug. "Sorry."

I couldn't care less about school, but I didn't want anyone else to suffer because I was a terrible student. Nox more than any of the rest of us had a decent chance of getting into college—assuming all the guys stopped hanging around the guys from Alpha Lupi.

"So, what the fuck did I just walk in on in there?" Ares

growled in my ear, not removing his arm from around my shoulders.

I tilted my head, only half-aware of the words actually spoken, as an insane urge to press my neck into his mouth hit me. "Nothing," I whined, my voice sounding foreign. "He was just asking about my grades, that's it."

Ares stepped back abruptly, just before the skin of my neck grazed his teeth. "Didn't seem like it."

I shook my head, trying to clear it. "You shouldn't challenge him like that," I muttered. "You're going to get hurt."

Ares snorted. "No, I'm not. I'm already bigger than him, and there's four of us."

"Well, forget hurt, then. You could get us kicked out."

That shut him right up.

We reached the car, and Ares unlocked it, jumping in the driver's side and starting it up. I opened the passenger side and got in while the other three guys piled in the back, just like we did every morning. The guys had done a ton of work on it, and it looked pretty good now. We were honestly just glad that the Wards hadn't sold it out from under us yet.

"Did you hear about Flora?" Killian asked as we pulled out of the driveway and headed off toward the school.

I turned around in my seat, grateful for a distraction from my burning face. "No, what about her?"

"She's gone."

I breathed a sigh of relief, then covered it as if I didn't know exactly what was going on. "What? Why?"

Flora Cabot had gone to our school ever since I'd lived at the Wards. She was popular because she came from one of the few rich families in town and had been going to senior parties since the eighth grade. I despised her.

"She's about to turn seventeen," Nox replied, as though it were obvious. "She should have been sent away long before now, but I think her parents were trying to have her finish out the school year."

"I didn't realize," I muttered.

I turned back around and sunk down in my seat, putting my face against the window's cool glass. Suddenly, I was even more insecure about her general existence. Not that it mattered. No one knew for sure she would present as an omega, and until then, she was no different from a beta, but that didn't stop her from using it to flirt with all the guys. Especially the alphas.

If she ended up presenting as a beta, the Institute would send her back. A jealous part of me wanted her to.

"How long until we know if she's coming back?" I asked, trying to sound casual.

"She won't," Rafe replied flatly.

"How do you know?" I said too fast.

I could tell from his tone he was raising an eyebrow at me. "She was tiny. She's definitely one. If we ever see her again, it will be on TV."

Killian barked a laugh, kicking the back of Ares' seat so hard the whole car shook. "Good thing you never fucked her."

My ears burned—right there was the sole reason I despised Flora. She'd been making a play for my guys for years. Petty? Yes, but I didn't care.

"I'm not a fucking idiot," Ares snapped, giving me a sideways look. "She was always going on about how she was probably an omega. I wouldn't risk going anywhere near her. "

I didn't comment. My skin itched with irritation knowing any kind of heat from an alpha could push an omega over the edge of transition. That Flora was willing to risk it just to be with my guys had my stomach turning over.

Normally, if there was even a chance that someone was an omega, they were sequestered away to a training facility to be trained for rich alphas. No celebrity alpha would want to mate an omega who had been scent bound.

Thank God for that, because there was no way I could survive losing my guys to an omega.

KILLIAN
FIVE

We pulled into the school parking lot, and Ares parked in our usual spot right out front. No one dared take it, even if we were close to twenty minutes late to first period. As a pack of alphas, we ruled this school, and everyone knew it.

I jumped out of the car and rushed around to Bliss' door, entwining our fingers as I hauled her out with enough force that she landed against my chest. She squealed in surprise but didn't step back.

Her sweet, flowery scent wrapped around us, and I dropped my nose, unable to stop myself from breathing her in. The way she curled her fingers into my chest told me she could feel my heart slamming into my rib cage.

"Good morning." Goose bumps ran down her neck as my breath grazed her ear. We hadn't had the chance to talk yet, and the distance was killing me. I pulled my head back, meeting her violet eyes, and nearly stuttered on my words. "Missed you." I punctuated it with a playful wink.

She stepped away from me, cheeks pink, but didn't let go of my hand. "I saw you last night."

Heat shot to my dick, and I had to adjust my pants. I desperately wanted to know how she tasted.

Ares shot me a look over Bliss' shoulder. "Get her to class."

I couldn't give a shit about class, but I tugged her hand, leading her into the school anyway. If we didn't hurry, Mr. Walsh would write Bliss up, and she'd hate that.

All eyes turned on us as we walked into the school, Ares on Bliss' other side and Nox and Rafe following behind. There was a hum of whispered words as students parted for us, pressing themselves against the walls, knowing better than to get in our space. I glowered at a kid who stared at Bliss a second too long, and the tangy, bitter taste of fear filled my mouth.

Good.

We walked directly to her class before the guys split off, Ares hesitating at the door. "Stay with her."

"Hell yeah." I smirked. I hadn't planned on letting Bliss go, but it helped that he was on board.

Ares took a step toward her, and she had to tip her head all the way back to meet his gaze. "I'll see you at lunch."

She swallowed before answering, voice a little shaky. "Yup. See you then."

Her scent filled the surrounding space, and I had to work hard to suppress my groan. She always smelled good, but this was more than that. Ares' gaze met mine, his brows pulled together. I shrugged. His guess was as good as mine.

The teacher did a double take as I strode into class but didn't say a word. Whatever. I didn't give a shit if I didn't belong here, so he shouldn't either.

Bliss walked to her spot a few rows in, where a guy took

up the seat beside her. I raised an eyebrow at the beta. He fumbled picking up his things, nearly dropping his books, and shifted a seat down.

The teacher droned on about mitochondria while I tuned him out, turning my attention to Bliss. Nox's sweater practically swallowed her, so big it hid her shorts. Her smooth, tanned skin on full display had my fingers twitching to run my fingers over it. I shifted until I barely brushed my leg against her and smiled at her sharp intake of breath.

Bliss flushed, pink rising to her cheeks. She firmly ignored me, which just taunted me to do it again. She pulled her hair up into a high ponytail, the baby hair around her neck damp with sweat. My girl was hot, and not just in the sexy way. With her neck exposed, nothing prevented her sweet, addictive scent from wrapping around me, and I shifted in closer until I pressed fully into her side. Her hooded gaze met mine, lip caught between her teeth. Fuck. An electric current burned through me as her tongue wet her lips. A low rumble formed in my chest. I was going to kiss her right here. Damn the consequences.

The guy in the seat in front of us turned around and leaned on Bliss' desk. "Hey."

"Hey?" She jumped, whipping her head up to meet his eyes.

My lust morphed into anger as his fingers brushed close to her arm. I racked my brain trying to come up with the guy's name. Jason, or maybe Jake. Who cared? He wasn't going to last long enough for her to say it. He glanced my way but quickly turned his eyes down.

That didn't stop him from opening his damn mouth. "Can I borrow a pencil?"

"Oh, sure." She let out a breath, sounding almost

relieved. I glared at him, my heart rate spiking. I didn't fucking like him.

She grabbed a pencil at random and tried to hand it to him without looking.

The idiot reached out, but instead of taking the pencil, he grabbed her hand, linking his fingers with hers, the pencil held awkwardly between them. A low growl of warning rumbled from my chest, and he snapped his hand back, looking a little dazed. He glanced between Bliss and me before saying, "Never mind."

The only thing stopping me from slamming his sandy-blond head into his desk was Bliss' worried gaze. *What the fuck was that?*

She looked at me, eyebrow raised. "You okay?"

I nodded. "Sure."

We moved through the morning like zombies. My irritation only got worse at the looks she was getting. Her skin had stayed flushed, and I raised my hand, rubbing my finger over her cheek. "You feeling alright?"

"Yeah, just warm." I had half a mind to tell her to take the sweater off, but then I really would bash someone's head for looking at her. She was tugging every protective instinct in me to the surface.

On the way to lunch, she sidestepped an overenthusiastic theater kid who was trying to talk to her about the upcoming show. I moved her to my other side and tucked her between me and the lockers. I swear, if one more person approached her—

"Hey, Bliss." Andrew, a guy from our history class, sidled up to her and put his arm against the closest locker, stopping her from moving forward. *Fucking dead man walking right here.*

"Er, hey." She glanced up at him as she stripped off her

sweatshirt, not even caring that now her tank top underneath was sweaty enough to be sticking to her skin like a wet T-shirt contest. I groaned and pulled her back firmly into my chest, dropping my chin to the crown of her head.

My voice dipped dangerously low when his gaze dropped to her chest. "Fuck off."

He took a step back, looking at me, but returned to Bliss. "What's up?" The dead man grinned at her.

"Nothing?" Her scent turned sour with suspicion.

In the entire time we'd been here, no one dared to disobey our order to stay away from her. Hanging out with four gigantic, terrifying alphas was one hell of a deterrent.

Her voice came out firm. Good girl. "You're blocking my way."

"What are you doing later?"

This guy has no survival instincts.

"Uh..." She opened her mouth, half-shocked and half-amused.

"We could go to a movie or something?" he continued.

I wrapped my arms around her middle, and she sighed, relaxing into me. "Dude, you're two seconds away from losing your teeth." I let the growl come through my words, and he blanched.

"Uh, no, just being friendly."

"Don't be," Nox said, coming up beside us. "She has friends. Fuck off."

Bliss tipped her head back, resting it on my chest, not caring that we chased off her potential date. A low purr silently rumbled through me, and she momentarily stiffened before relaxing further into my embrace.

I smirked as Andrew turned tail and scampered back down the hallway, giving the impression of a deer lucky to have escaped an apex predator. Bliss didn't bother watching him go. Instead, she turned to Nox smiling. "That's one way to do it."

He smirked and took in her features. She was even more flushed, sweat dampening her skin. Nox took one look at me, sensing my restlessness. "How's your morning going?"

"You don't want to know," I grunted. It was now two random guys that came on to her. I clenched my teeth from the force of possessiveness I was feeling. She let her full weight lean against me, and Nox's brows pinched together. She seemed weaker than normal.

Something was off with our girl. Nox growled low, the sounds reverberating in me. I loosened my grip, letting him pull her against him, but I didn't let go of her hips.

Nox rubbed the back of his neck, looking highly conflicted. Then, the taste of smoke and honey filled my mouth, and his arm wrapped around her, pulling her tight, forcing me to let go. I smiled at the sound of his groan. The bastard was against us telling her everything and letting this play out. It was good for him to crave what he was demanding we couldn't have.

"Maybe we should bail for the rest of the day," he said, looking down at her outfit—or lack thereof.

Hell yeah, I was down for that.

She tilted her head, staring up at him with hooded violet eyes. "Are you serious? You never skip."

Nox's gaze caught on her mouth, and his chest rose and fell like he'd just run a marathon. He took a deep through his nose, and his voice came out on a groan. "Dead serious."

A huge crowd of soccer players moved past us, shouting and running. As if slapped in the face, Nox jolted away from her. His eyes narrowed slightly, and he took another deep breath through his nose. Brows pinched together, he said, "Yeah... never mind. Come on."

He kept more distance than usual between them as we walked down the hall in the cafeteria's direction. Like everything else in the school, it was about thirty years out of date and falling apart at the seams. The yellowed, round tables and chipped linoleum floor definitely didn't say "appetizing" any more than the substandard food. Still, there wasn't really anywhere else we were allowed to hang out.

We made a beeline for our usual table. As we approached, I could swear his eyes followed her more than usual, and God knew I'd been paying attention.

We'd put the word out to stay the hell away from her, and no one had crossed that line. There weren't a lot of alphas in town—at least, not teenage ones. Since omegas were dying out and alphas only came from alpha-omega parents, you just didn't see a ton of non-beta kids in low-income areas. We didn't know who our parents were, but it was a safe bet they were all either the product of infidelity or some kind of gang environment, born to parents who wouldn't or couldn't keep us.

Nox sat down at the table across from Bliss, a smile tipping his lips. "You look flushed."

I sat beside her, and she rested on my side. She yawned. "I'm burning up, but I feel fine otherwise."

Nox leaned over the table and ran a finger over her cheek. "Yeah?"

"Mmmhmmm." She purred at his touch. The sound had him practically crawling over the table before a cough nearby had him sit back down. We couldn't be seen as too friendly. People were used to our touching by now, but there were always going to be rumors about us. We were careful not to give any proof they were true.

He scanned his phone, seeming to relax. No doubt

texting the rest of the crew. "Few more classes, then we can get out of here."

If he knew the half of it, he wouldn't take that bored tone.

His gaze stayed glued to his phone, even as his body turned toward her. The bastard was doing his best to stay distracted.

Bliss' soft voice caught his attention. "What are you looking at?"

He flipped his phone around to show her. It was some kind of build-a-castle game. "I'm winning, see?"

She frowned, twirling one strand of blonde-and-purple hair around her finger. "Since when do you have data for stuff like that?"

My smile turned a little forced, answering for him. "Come on, B. You know we don't want you involved in that stuff."

She tapped her fingers against the table in agitation, gaze turned away, not happy with that answer. We tried to keep this stuff away from her. Anyone with eyes could see we were a good investment from a recruiting perspective, and for all we knew, we had blood family in the life.

"Hey, Bliss."

I snapped my head up at the same time as Nox. The figure of one of the soccer players loomed behind her.

"Er, hi," she replied.

Across from me, Nox growled audibly. "Who are you?"

"Hey, man." The kid's voice got far less confident speaking to Nox, but I had to give it to him—he was ballsy. "So, um, Bliss. Is this seat taken?"

"Excuse me?" she spluttered, shocked.

Talking to her was one thing, but no one sat with us.

Ever. Nox and I gaped at each other, taken aback for a full beat as the guy sat down on the other side of her.

"Yeah, it's very much taken," she said quickly, trying to scoot away from the soccer player. "Sorry."

He tried to reach for her arm. "Aw, don't be like that."

My hand shot out and grabbed the soccer player's wrist, twisting hard. "Don't touch."

The guy yelped and scrambled to his feet as rage poured through me.

"What the fuck is this?" Ares' harsh voice boomed through the cafeteria, and I jerked my head up, smirking.

'Bout fucking time.

Ares strode down the center of the room, Rafe slightly behind him. Rage rolled off them in waves to the point where everyone in the room had to feel it.

For half a second, I thought he was only talking about the guy at our table now cradling his hand, but then I saw his icy eyes were fixed on the rest of the soccer players loitering just to our right. The guys—all betas but big for their designation—were right there waiting to back up their friend, and they were all staring *right at Bliss.*

"Do you want to keep your eyes?" Ares barked at the soccer players, using the full force of the power behind that statement. It tasted like iron.

In the back of the room, a girl burst into tears, and out of the corner of my eye, I saw a beta teacher retreat into a classroom and shut the door. *At least they remember why they don't fuck with us.*

I looked around us, expecting everyone to be cowering away. Surprise filled me when I realized they were getting closer. *What the hell?*

Bliss shifted in her seat, and without thinking, I ran my

nose up her neck. A groan caught in the back of my throat. Her floral smell filled my nose, and my hands gripped her waist. I burrowed my face in her neck again, my teeth aching.

"Holy shit," Rafe said, his eyes growing wide. "We need to get out of here."

Ares and Nox nodded silently at each other.

"Why?" she asked at the same time she turned her neck, exposing it fully to me. I opened my mouth, my teeth aching to graze over her soft skin. Sudden clarity hit me, and I scrambled back so fast I nearly hit the ground.

Bliss' eyes met mine, hurt and confusion filling them. "What's going on?"

There was a long pause before I answered, "Probably nothing, baby."

"I have work later," she protested.

"No, you don't," Rafe laughed darkly as we steered her toward the double doors of the school.

She dug her heels in, refusing to move. "No, wait. What the hell is going on?"

All four of us turned in unison to face her. She was framed against the sunlit entrance to the school. The sun cast a fuzzy halo around her as she stared us down, almost too perfect to be real. Her eyes turned heated, and she bit down on her bottom lip, making the softest of whimpering sounds.

Four growls tore through the silence, and I shuddered as heat drove through me, practically yelling at me to take her.

Ares ran his hands through his hair. "Fuck."

The tires screeched along the road as Ares turned the corner near our clearing. All four boys shouted over each other in a dull, unintelligible roar. Anxiety licked up my spine, and I shifted in my seat. What the hell was going on?

Nox's hand dashed to grab mine, running his thumb over the sensitive skin on my wrist. My gaze traced his face. A line stood out between his brows, and his hair stood straight up from where he'd repeatedly run his fingers through it. He squeezed my hand and shifted his face to look out the window. "It's okay, Bliss."

It didn't feel okay.

For once, I had been relegated to the back seat instead of the passenger seat as usual. Ares avoided my gaze in the rearview mirror as Killian beat out a frantic drumbeat on the dash beside him. While Nox seemed afraid to let me go, by contrast, Rafe had moved as far away from me as possible, keeping his nose pressed to the window.

If they didn't tell me what was going on soon, I was going to scream.

The car slammed to an abrupt halt in the tiny parking lot on the edge of the park, and my seat belt dug into my chest. I yelped when it pinched my skin.

"Fucking, Christ." Nox removed my seat belt and ran his thumb over the small purple line on my chest. A low, menacing growl emanated from his throat when his glare whipped up to Ares. "What the hell were you thinking?"

I tilted my head to the side. The mark had already disappeared. "I'm fine, calm down."

My words were lost. Ares was already up and out of the car, ripping my door open, and he hauled me out. He crowded me until my back pressed against the trunk, and his head dipped down to rest against my forehead. A too-sweet smell filled the air, and I tasted worry on my tongue, like dying flowers. Piercing blue eyes lingered on the sore spot before meeting my gaze. "I'm sorry, Bliss."

I lifted my hand to his face and ran my thumb over Ares' sharp cheekbone. "You're acting weird."

Killian slipped his hand in mine, interlacing our fingers, and pulled me from under Ares. "We just need to get to the clearing, baby, where no one can hear us. Then we can talk about everything."

I pushed past him on the trail, stomping my feet with each step. My patience ran dangerously low being kept in the dark like this. Their footsteps tore after me, the air filling with citrus and bitterness. Like unsweetened cranberry lemonade.

Crossing the clearing, I turned to glare at them. I put my hands on my hips. "Start talking."

Four boys stood in front of me. My boys.

Their eyes snapped to mine, and I had to take a step

back as a tangy, bitter taste filled my mouth. Fear. It tasted like fear. My feet stumbled back as the realization hit me: I was tasting their emotions...and I'd been doing it for days. The world spun.

"But...that's crazy. Betas can't smell emotions," I said, more to myself than to them.

Rafe leapt forward and caught me, pulling me into his chest. "It's going to be okay, Bliss. I promise it's going to be okay." His arms bound tight around me, and I took gulping sips of his familiar scent, letting him soothe me with each passing breath.

My legs solidified beneath me, but I didn't pull away from the safety of Rafe's arms. My body craved his strength, and by the way his arms tightened, it didn't feel like he'd let me go. I turned my head against Rafe's chest, looking into Ares' electric-blue eyes. "What's happening?"

Ares had always been the most opinionated and dominant of our group. Now though, he looked like he would have happily passed that job to anyone else. He rubbed his palms over his eyes, then slowly met my gaze. "You know what's happening, Omega."

The world seemed to tip on its side. Rafe's powerful arms held me up, even as my knees threatened to buckle again. He whispered reassuring words I couldn't make out into my hair.

"That can't be right." I should be ecstatic to be an omega. It was every girl's dream. Instead, the same tangy, bitter taste filled the surrounding air. What did it mean for me? For us? "Have any of you ever met an omega?" I asked, almost desperately.

Killian laughed, and my gaze flew to him. He'd perched on the arm of the threadbare sofa, his head in his hands. "It's right. I've never been more positive of anything."

"I don't understand. My mom was a beta."

Nox stepped forward, his hair more red than brown in this light. "We don't know either. We never knew who your dad was. Male omegas are even rarer than female ones, but they're out there."

I sucked in a breath. It was possible, but... "Why would an omega sleep with a beta?"

Killian's eyes met mine. "Probably to avoid asshole alphas during their heat."

The trees swirled around me as my vision blurred. Ares barked, the dominance in his voice filling the space. "Put her on the couch."

Rafe turned us so he sat down on the sofa cushion first and pulled me onto his lap with him. Something in the back of my mind fought against my helplessness, but I couldn't pull myself out of it. I kept my eyes closed, head tucked into his chest.

I was about to become an omega. A flipping omega. How the hell had no one ever noticed? How had I not known? If anyone had guessed there was even the slightest chance of this, I'd have been ripped from the home and sent to the Institute immediately, just like Flora from our high school.

Shit. The Institute.

I jolted up from Rafe's arms, and everyone stared at me. My voice sounded weak to my ears. "I don't want to go to the Institute."

Their muscles tensed like they were holding themselves back, as if my worry physically pained them. *Oh. Of course it's literally upsetting them because they can smell it.*

Suddenly, so many things became more clear. There was a vast difference between being intellectually aware that alphas were different from betas and experiencing the difference firsthand. It had never been more clear to me that my friends and I weren't the same. *Except, actually, now we kind of are.* I was going to pass out.

No one spoke for a full minute, and tension pulled tight in the clearing. I turned toward Ares, but his head was down, supported by his hands, elbows on his knees. Dread tightened like a band over my chest. I didn't want to leave, but did they want me to? "Ares?"

His nostrils flared, and his gaze snapped to mine. "I should tell you to go. You'll mate some rich alpha and live in a giant house near a lake and never have to worry about anything ever again. You deserve that." He took a breath. I hated every word. "But I can't. I'm too fucking selfish to let you go."

My breath caught in my chest, warring with my frantically beating heart. *Oh my God.*

Ares's eyes darted around to the rest of the guys, all nodding with him. "It's got to be your decision. You've got to tell us to let you go, Bliss. We can't do it on our own."

"My decision?" A laugh escaped my mouth, but it was missing the lightness it usually held. I could hardly breathe. "Are you serious?"

"Bliss, look." Nox looked like he was going to crack a back tooth from clenching his jaw. "You should at least consider it. The Institute only mates omegas to celebrities and government officials and shit like that. You literally just won the lottery."

Pain sliced through me, and I flinched involuntarily. "Why would you even say that?"

Nox shook his head, his eyes pleading. "We're all really young. If you go to be trained now, they'd put you on blockers for a few years. None of this has to start right away."

I gazed around the circle incredulously, my vision blurring. "Why are you trying to talk me into this? They can take their fancy houses and prudish alphas and shove it. You're my pack."

The space filled with their growls, and my blood sang in my veins in response. Rafe spun me in his arms, and his hand gripped me delicately around my jaw, only hard enough to keep me in place. "We're just trying to make sure you understand. You know once you present as an omega, there's no turning back. You'll be stuck with us."

The words filled me with such relief that I collapsed against his chest. Omegas were scent bound with whoever scented their perfume when they'd fully transitioned into an omega.

Whether that be a single alpha or a pack of them. That's why it was safer for young omegas to be sent to the Institute. They'd be placed on blockers all the way until the Institute found someone "appropriate," in other words, "rich," to be mated to an omega.. Suddenly, I counted down the seconds until my perfume came in and our pack became official.

"Give her to us," Nox said, and Rafe handed me over to him.

He and Rafe must've switched places, because Nox's and Killian's scents surrounded me, merging until it became a delicious medley. Killian's hand ran up and down my legs as Nox ran circles up my back, his mouth peppering barely there kisses on my collarbone. A shiver ran through me, and warmth pooled between my thighs. I whimpered, and four matching growls responded to my call. Thick need filled the space and pulsed around us.

A new sickening smell hit my senses. I tasted the air, still new at being able to sense emotions. My chest caved, realizing what it was: sadness.

"What if we can't protect you?" Killian's voice was so low it nearly covered the fact it was shaking.

"She'll be fine," Ares growled. "Don't even talk like that."

"Come on, man," Killian said. "Have you ever heard of a teenage pack with an omega? Even a really famous one? Fuck no. It's too dangerous."

Anger stung my chest, and I made a growling noise of my own. "Well, I'm not going anywhere, so we'll have to figure it out."

Everyone moved closer to me, compelled to give an omega what she wanted. Nox was the first to speak. "We need a plan. We need to find somewhere to lie low."

"We can't go home," Ares said, his eyes glued to me.

"Why?" I whined, surprising myself with how needy my voice sounded.

My face grew hotter, the warmth traveling all the way down my body as the taste of the air shifted. All eyes snapped to me again, expressions shifting from worry to obvious hunger.

Nox groaned and shifted slightly away from me. "That's why. We can't just parade an unmarked omega out in the open. People will riot."

"I knew something was off this morning," Ares said, more to himself than to me. "You can't go anywhere near Ward like this, even if you haven't fully presented yet. Any alpha in a five-mile radius will recognize an omega in transition."

My eyes grew wide. *Oh.*

So many things were hitting me so fast. It hadn't even registered that the guys weren't the only alphas who would be interested in me.

"Mr. Ward is mated," I pointed out.

Rafe crossed his arms, making meaningful eye contact with Ares across the circle. "Better not risk it."

"Fine. Then where are we supposed to go?"

There was an extremely long beat of silence where no one seemed to know what to say. I glanced around. I was not excited about sleeping out here, even if we were all together.

"Let's get a hotel," Killian said, shrugging.

I was about to ask if they even had the money for a hotel, but it didn't matter anyway.

"We can't," Rafe replied. "Too many people."

Ares stood and started pacing, his hands in his white hair. I'd never seen him so agitated.

"What about the warehouse downtown?" Nox sounded unenthusiastic. "Almost no one knows about it, and no one will be within scenting distance."

Rafe's head snapped up. "Nah, everyone knows about it."

I looked around. I didn't know who "everyone" was, but I was willing to bet it was the gang they weren't really supposed to be a part of. This was just another one of their secrets.

Ares' razor-sharp teeth pierced his lip as he nodded. "I'm almost positive no one will be in there tonight. We'll have to figure something else out tomorrow."

"Where would we go?" The question was out of my mouth before I could stop it. I didn't want to put any reason out there that would change their minds.

Ares replied quickly, "Doesn't matter. We'll figure it out together."

The warehouse was an enormous open space. There were no walls to block the view from one end to the other, and only a few crates lined one side, but other than that, it was pretty much empty. The building was old, paint peeling from the steel walls, and the windows were covered in film, making it impossible for anyone passing by to look inside. Not that we expected any company.

"What is this place used for?" I muttered. "There's nothing in here."

"There's shit in here when there has to be," Ares said vaguely, exchanging a glance with Rafe. "We're going to grab stuff from the car. We'll be right back."

My skin prickled as I surveyed the space. My body whined. I didn't like it here. It was too big and too cold. "I liked the fire pit better, honestly."

Warm arms banded around my middle and spun me against Killian's hard chest.

His head dropped beside my head, and his soft breath fanned across my neck. "You can't sleep outside, B."

His alpha scent calmed my jittering nerves, and I leaned into him. They'd always been able to calm me, but this was different. It was on an instinctual level to let them take care of me.

"We can feel your anxiety. Tell us what you need."

My gaze shifted around the warehouse, and a shudder ran through me. Nox stepped in close to us, his heat warming my back. I relaxed, liking the feeling of being surrounded by them. His chest vibrated through me. "She needs a nest."

I gasped at his words. Like a good alpha, he was already more attuned to what I needed before I was. They slowly peeled away from me, and I made a pained sound at the back of my throat. Killian's forehead dropped to mine, but he didn't close the inches of space between us. "Let us take care of this."

I straightened. I refused to let my instincts get the better of me and took a step back. "Of course."

Ares and Rafe walked through the entry door, carrying blankets and the clearing's sofa cushions with them.

The boys dragged the crates from along the wall to one corner and boxed it off into a small room-like space with them. They used the cushions from our couch to line the floor, creating a makeshift bed. There weren't any pillows, but they'd brought all the throw blankets from the clearing. I pulled a blanket to my nose, all of their scents surrounding me, and made a distinct omega hum of satisfaction.

Nox gestured to the space, and a too-sweet taste coated my tongue. "I'm sorry it's not better."

I shook my head and focused my attention on him. "It's perfect."

Rafe walked straight to me, pulled me into his arms, and dropped to the floor, dragging me with him. His nose ran up the side of my neck as he breathed me in, growling low in his chest.

I hummed and tilted my head to the side, exposing my neck to him. He placed gentle nips there, a low rumble against my back.

Ares appeared on my other side, running his tongue along my collarbone like he did it every day. "Tomorrow, we'll slip into the group home and grab our stuff. Tonight, we'll stay here."

"Mmmhmm," I said.

I probably would have agreed to anything right now. They could have asked me to commit murder, and I would have happily gone along with it.

"Fuck, she's close to heat." Rafe's words against my skin brought me back to attention. I couldn't tell from his tone if he was excited or worried.

Ares and Rafe pulled back abruptly from either side of my neck, and I whined at the loss of contact. I snapped my mouth shut. The omega was coming closer to the surface as my presenting approached. I'd grown up thinking I was a beta. I'd never prepared for this transition. Being an omega was more primal, more wild than I expected.

Every omega went into heat as soon as they presented. Heat meant something different for omegas. Their bodies were vulnerable when it took over them. It's why the Institute took precautions to keep them safe by having them on blockers until they were mated off to rich men capable of protecting them. I didn't believe for a second protection was why those men mated. No, it was the status it brought them. Omegas were rare, and mating one meant you were above everyone else.

Killian crawled across the cushions toward us. He grabbed for me, and Ares and Rafe didn't protest—that seemed like a good sign to me. I wasn't all that familiar with omega pack dynamics. The last thing I wanted was for them to start fighting, but at least with us, that didn't seem like a concern.

Nox reached over to where Killian held me between his knees and ran his fingers across my face. "I hate to be the voice of reason here, but she needs blockers."

"Why?" I asked. Now that I'd gotten a taste of this, I didn't want to go back to being regular.

They seemed to be having some kind of silent argument with their eyes over my head. If I had any experience with reading the smell of emotions in the room, I would probably have a better sense of what was going on, but as it was, all I was getting was the heavy odor of dead lilies and pennies.

"He's right, B," Killian said finally. "You can't present right now. Not until we have a better plan and a safer place for you to stay."

Intellectually, I could understand what they meant. I was still in the transitional stage, but if I presented and went into heat, then that could last for days. The irrational, animalistic part of my brain didn't care though. I wanted them to claim me. Now.

That thought must have triggered some kind of emotional response because growls erupted around the circle. Their combined scents overtook me, and my stomach warmed.

Killian shuffled back, a low growl rumbling in the back of his throat. "Yup. We need to get those blockers fast."

I sighed, defeated. My mouth tasted sour—the guys looked as unhappy about that as I was.

A yawn took over my face, and my eyes drooped. Today

was long, and tomorrow would be more of the same. I shifted up the bed until I could lie out fully. All of their eyes were on me like a weighted blanket, but they didn't move to join. I'd probably made them nervous.

"Will you sleep with me?"

That's all it took to be surrounded by them, Nox on my left, with Rafe behind him, and Killian on my right, followed by Ares. I knew they were concerned about not being able to protect me, but I'd never felt as safe as I did right now.

The following morning, I woke in a pile of limbs. Sun streamed through the plastic-covered windows of the warehouse, and I burrowed under someone's arm to try to shield my face from the light. I'd never thought I would miss my bed at the group home, but my canopy was pretty cozy. Wherever the guys and I ended up, we would have to get something like that.

Nox shifted against my back, and I craned my neck to look at him. He had one arm thrown over my hip, and behind him, Ares had his long arm wrapped around both of us. I smiled. I liked the closeness with all of them like this. In any of my fantasies of all of us together, I'd never imagined I'd get this lucky.

The arm covering half my face twitched, and Rafe shifted to look at me. "Are you okay?"

"Never better," I yawned.

In some ways, that was true. Yesterday was a blur. Like a scene out of someone else's life and I was just visiting. Nox had probably said it best—I'd essentially just won the genetic lottery, and now I got to share my win with all my best friends. It was almost too good to be true.

What made this so crazy was how rare omegas were. I'd heard that there used to be lots of them, but due to war, famine, and selective breeding, omegas now made up only about two percent of the population. The Omega Institute was a relatively new government program set up to combat the problem, but it was far from a perfect system.

Killian's head popped up over Rafe's shoulder, and he grinned. "I, for one, slept great."

Ares growled. "My hip hurts. We're getting an actual bed tonight."

I couldn't help grinning. I didn't care where we were—this was perfect.

A sweet, fruity smell filled the air as happiness bloomed in my chest, and everyone shifted around me. Nox twisted his fingers in the back of my hair, running his nose up the column of my neck. "We're running out of time."

I rolled over until I was half on top of Nox's chest, looking down into his green gaze. I gave him a small smile. "You keep trying to turn me off."

Ares grabbed the back of my neck with surprising strength and forced me to turn my head to look at him. He leaned close so he was speaking against my mouth. "You're lucky one of us is half-rational, Love. Be grateful."

I whined, my teeth aching to open up and bite his lip. It was right there. I didn't want to be grateful—I wanted to say screw it and just do this. Now.

The flowery smell took on a spicy taste. Like jasmine, honey, and chili peppers.

"Cut that shit out," Rafe barked at Ares, who dropped me and flopped back down against the cushions.

My spine went straight at the dominant note in Rafe's voice. "Sorry."

"Don't be sorry, baby," Killian said. "We just need to

make sure we get you blockers ASAP, or we're going to have bigger problems."

"We can steal some," Nox said, keeping his eyes firmly fixed on the ceiling, as though trying not to look at me.

"Okay," Ares said, back to all business. "We'll go there and then back to the house to get our stuff."

"And then what?" I asked.

Killian reached across Rafe and ran a hand through my hair. "Dunno, baby, but we're going to take care of you no matter what."

The guys argued for a full five minutes about if it was safer to keep the windows down in the car so they could breathe or keep them closed so no one else would scent me. I watched with alarmed fascination.

This was so not my world.

Potential omegas spent years in training so they would have a good idea of the culture and what to expect. I was totally lost, guided exclusively by animal instinct.

Nox wrapped his arms around my waist, holding me tightly to him, even as he argued with Killian about how we all needed to maintain distance from each other. The cognitive dissonance of that action told me the guys were equally rattled by this whole thing, even if they were hiding it better.

Finally, we all piled into the car and sped down Main Street in the direction of the center of town. I leaned my head against the passenger-side window, thankful for the cool glass against my burning skin. I was burning up from the inside out. "How long will it take to get those pills?"

"Not long." Rafe threw me a glance in the rearview mirror. "They always have them at the free clinic."

My eyes widened. "Do I have to go in?"

"Fuck no," Ares snapped as he skidded through a barely yellow light.

"Drop me off there," Nox said. "I'll get the stuff and meet you back at the house."

Ares nodded in silent agreement, and I sank lower in my seat, pressing my knees together. This was a lot of drama over just me. All I could hope for was that soon things would calm down and we could all be together for real.

ARES

EIGHT

I held my breath as I sped down a heavily settled suburban street in the direction of the group home. Some old lady waved at me to slow down as we whipped past, and I flipped her off. *Do not test me today.*

"Please don't kill us," Bliss said from the seat beside me.

I growled involuntarily at that image and eased off the gas. The sweet taste of her satisfaction filled the car, and I forced myself not to inhale.

Rafe met my eyes in the rearview mirror, and his brows arched. I knew he was thinking the same thing I was: *This is fucking crazy.*

Two days ago, I would have done anything for Bliss—any of us would have. Today, that was still true, but it was like I didn't have a choice anymore. Not that I was complaining—it was just uncomfortable not to be in control of your own body.

I turned onto our road and slowed to a near crawl. All we needed was for Ward to hear us and come out to investigate. I ground my teeth. "We'll run in and grab some of our stuff. You stay in the car."

Bliss looked up at me with wide, violet eyes. "I need to pack though, especially if we're not coming back."

"We've got it," Killian said from the back seat, reaching forward to twist the end of her hair around his fingers.

She huffed out an annoyed breath, and I warred with myself over giving her what she wanted and keeping her safe. Safe won out.

I pulled into the driveway, my heart beating fast with pent-up adrenaline. There weren't any other cars here, but that didn't mean anything. Someone was always hanging around the group home.

I leaned across the center console and grabbed Bliss's chin, tipping it up. "We'll be right back. Stay here, Love."

Love. I couldn't remember when I started calling her that, but it was accurate. I'd loved her since I was six years old. Beta or omega, there was never going to be anyone else.

"But—" she started to say.

I could see the exact moment she got distracted. Her pupils dilated, and the honey smell of her arousal hit me all at once. *Fuck.*

"Ares." Rafe kicked my seat. "Let's go."

I wrenched myself away and slammed the car door without another word. If Nox didn't get back soon with those blockers, this was going to fucking kill me.

"You've got to stop touching her," Rafe muttered as we jogged up the porch steps. "You're making it worse."

I barked a laugh. "You're one to talk. You set this off in the first place."

He came to an abrupt halt with his hand on the front door, and Killian slammed into his back. "Dude, what the fuck?"

Rafe ignored him. "What do you mean I set this off?"

I glanced around. *Do we really need to be talking about this now? On the fucking porch? No.* "The other night, you clearly triggered it. Now, come on."

Rafe fell too quiet as we moved up the stairs toward the room the four of us had shared for the last decade. I had no idea what his deal was. Everyone knew you had to keep potential omegas away from alphas, or it would trigger their heats. Of course, we hadn't known Bliss was an omega, but it didn't matter now anyway.

I stuffed a bunch of clothes and shit into a bag and then moved on to Bliss's room, Killian close behind me. I almost laughed. We both stood there and stared at the nest she had created around her bed. "How did we not put two and two together?"

Killian chuckled. "We're idiots—"

His words cut off abruptly, and the hair on the back of my neck lifted. Sight, sound, and smell came into focus. Killian's eyes were wide, and his muscles clenched in his jaw as he sucked in through his nose. A bitter, tangy taste turned the air acrid. Blood rushed in my ears, blocking out the words Killian was shouting as the smell of fear swelled until it burned my nose.

Bliss.

Rafe darted out of our room, thundering after me down the stairs and out the door. My heart beat against my ribs, and my blood boiled as the metallic taste of panic filled my mouth. I whipped my head around, searching for the source of the smell.

The bitter smell of Bliss's fear permeated the air all around me as I tore down the porch steps and across the yard toward her muffled screams.

No.

Ward had Bliss pressed up against the side of the car, one hand around her throat and the other trying to tear at the belt of her shorts. A red haze came over my vision, and I charged forward, a growl tearing from my throat.

Nox ran up the driveway, reaching Ward first. He grabbed Ward by the back of the neck and tore him off Bliss, throwing him to the ground with enough force that he sunk into the grass a couple of inches.

"You boys think you can keep her safe?" Ward started to get up. "You think I'll be the only alpha to figure this out? To come after her?"

Rafe slammed his fist into Ward's mouth, snapping his head back as he dropped to his ass.

The corner of Ward's lips tipped up, and he spit blood onto the ground before wiping his mouth. He looked toward where Nox and Killian held Bliss between them. "She needs men who can protect her. Not boys who want to fuck her."

I grabbed him by the collar and pulled him onto his knees. "Men like you?"

Ward shook his head. "It's only a matter of time before some sick bastard kills you all and gets his hands on her."

"We'll protect her better than you could." My fist clenched at my sides, and I did my best to block out his words. I wouldn't let him get into my head.

"Oh yeah? What happens when those thugs you hang out with find out you're hiding an omega?"

I paused, chest heaving as I stared at Ward, then slammed my fist into his face until the asshole laid flat out on the grass.

My eyes found Bliss, shaking by the car. If I believed in omens or that kind of shit, this wasn't a good one.

We drove in silence until I spotted a rest station and pulled in, desperate to catch my breath. Ward's blood smeared my steering wheel where it had covered my hands, but no one commented. This felt like the kind of thing we wouldn't bring up again after today.

"Here, Little Wolf." Nox shoved a pill bottle at Bliss, the capsules rattling like a bass drum in the silent car.

She held them up to the light. "I need water."

I glanced back at the rest stop convenience store. It was run-down, just like everything else in this town, but it at least looked open. "Killian, go grab her a water."

"Can you see if they have a bathroom key too?" Bliss asked. "I just need a second..."

"No, you can't get out of the car," Rafe said too loudly.

Bliss snorted. "Well then, we're going to get really comfortable with each other really fast. It looks like a single-stall bathroom. I'll be fine."

I glanced at Nox, who usually had the most rational opinion on shit like...well, not like this—this was fucking crazy—but on other things. He was just rational in general.

"Just hurry," Nox said.

It was only a minute before Killian was back, and he handed the bottle of water and bathroom key to Bliss. "Take your pills."

She smirked, jumping out before we could stop her.

We got out of the car and waited. My eyes darted back and forth toward the door where Bliss had disappeared the moment she went into the bathroom. I didn't like this. "One of us should have gone with her."

Nox opened his mouth like he was going to tell me to calm down and then closed it again, clearly thinking better of it.

"Okay, so, where to?" Killian said, doing his best to keep the mood light.

For once, I had no answers. Rafe and I looked at each other, both hoping the other would come up with something. We all knew this was bad. Really fucking bad.

Rafe's gaze traveled over to the closed bathroom door and then back to me. "We need to be fucking real about this. We can't keep her with us."

An involuntary growl erupted from my chest, and I took a step forward. "What the fuck does that mean?"

Nox reached for my shoulder, trying to pull me back, but I shook him off. "Didn't you hear Ward? More alphas will be after her."

"I don't care. She's ours," I barked.

"Get your head out of your ass. You think you could protect her if someone else tried to take her?" Rafe spit the words at me.

I held up my bloody hand, waving it at Rafe and Nox. "Were you not watching just now?"

Killian stepped up behind me, seeming unsure what side of this argument he wanted to be on. I was about to lose my fucking shit on all of them—no one was making any sense.

"Ward is nothing," Rafe said. "If this happened in five years, yeah, no problem, but right now, we're going to get fucking killed, and Bliss will end up passed around Alpha Lupi or some other gang circuit for the rest of her life."

"So you're saying you wouldn't die to protect her," Killian growled at Rafe.

I stepped back to stand next to him, wholeheartedly agreeing with that statement.

"Fuck no," Nox growled back. "I'm saying she shouldn't

have to watch us all die and then get taken anyway. Ward was right about one thing: we can't protect her."

My chest caved as the weight of his words sank in. We'd be picked off one by one only to eventually leave her alone with whoever managed to kill us. "Do you have a better idea? Because all I fucking care about is keeping her safe," I snapped.

I couldn't believe we were even having this conversation. What the hell else were we supposed to do? Our options narrowed to a single fixed point the moment that Bliss had started transitioning.

"We could call the Institute," Nox said quietly.

He always was the smart one. I just wished he'd figured out a better way.

"Fuck." Killian slammed his fist against the trunk.

Rafe held up his phone and met each of our gazes. "I'm calling."

My heart was being ripped out of my chest, but I forced myself to nod. We said we'd save her even if it killed us. This just wasn't the type of death I had imagined.

The door to the rest stop bathroom opened, and Bliss looked toward where Rafe paced talking on the phone, just out of hearing distance. She sniffed the air when she got to us and tucked herself into Killian's arms. He pulled her tight to his chest, and his jaw clenched as he fought an inner battle.

Bliss' gaze darted between us, and her brows pinched together. "What's going on?"

Rafe jogged up to us, saving me from having to respond. "We're waiting for someone."

It was like we were waiting for a train wreck to happen, each second ticking down closer to the inevitable crash.

Nox stepped up to her, running his nose along her neck

and placing a slow kiss to her temple. Killian did the same on her other side, murmuring soft words I couldn't make out. She looked right between them, like she was meant to be there.

Not for much longer. I clenched my teeth, and a rumble of a growl escaped my throat at how fucking bullshit this all was.

Bliss' head snapped to me. She ran her thumb over my bottom lip. "Stop frowning at me like that. I'm fine. Plus, now we don't have to worry about Ward anymore. Right?"

My lip burned where she touched it, and I couldn't stop myself from running my tongue over her thumb. She tasted like jasmine and honey, and this was my last chance to kiss her. My mind went blank as instincts took over.

I closed the distance between us in half a step and crashed my mouth over hers, swallowing her whimpering sounds and sucking her air into my lungs. Blood rushed through my ears, drowning out everything else as I focused entirely on Bliss. I needed to burn this kiss into my memory to replay later when I was at my worst. When I would have turned to her, but now she would be gone.

Fuck. I didn't want to let her go, and I needed some part of her to know that.

I deepened the kiss, owning every part of her—stamping myself in her mind, begging her to remember me. Her fingers clung to my shirt, nails biting into my chest. Her soft moans turned wild as she lost control in my arms. An electric current sparked over my skin as the rich scent of her slick, jasmine and honey, filled my nose, my chest, my mind until my mind went blank except for one word. *Mine.*

Her eyes dilated, and my shoulders dropped as her scent dissipated in the air. Scent bonded.

I jerked back, shock trickling through me as she leaned

in closer, chasing the broken kiss. Three need-filled groans circled around us. Their dark gazes pinned on our girl, as if they'd just discovered the secret to happiness and she was standing right in front of them.

"Jesus fucking Christ." Killian's voice was weak, barely above a whisper.

Bliss opened her eyes and smiled at us as she fully became an omega, her scent bonding us forever. My eyes met Rafe's over Bliss's shoulder, then darted to Killian and Nox. Their expressions were equally shocked as they processed the bond slamming into place.

"Fuck." Nox ripped the water bottle from Killian's hand and shoved pills at Bliss. She looked at him, and a sadness tinted the air.

Rafe's voice barked out the command. "Take it."

He wasn't asking—the alpha demand came through loud and clear, and she had no choice but to obey. But it was too fucking late...and we all knew it. No blockers in the world could fix this now.

Instant regret hit me. Fuck. "Rafe, how long until—"

I didn't get a chance to finish my question.

Killian's crisp smell of lemon and vanilla swirled with Nox's smooth sandalwood, Rafe's peppers and coffee beans, and Ares' cloudless night sky. An overwhelming sense of rightness sank into my bones as each of their bonds snapped broken pieces of me back into place.

Strangled voices shouted around me, but as if I was underwater, I couldn't make out the words.

I leaned toward Ares like a plant seeking sunlight, and a smile stretched across my face, so wide my cheeks hurt. I met Ares' conflicted gaze, and my smile fell as a bitter taste tainted their bonds. Before I could even try to process the torment there, pills and a water bottle were thrust into my hands.

"Take them." Nox's bark was a slap in the face.

No. I didn't want to take them. I'd lose everything I was feeling, and he knew it, but the coercion of his bark wouldn't allow for any argument.

My hand moved of its own accord, bringing the blockers

to my mouth. Theoretically, I understood why I needed to hide my omega scent, but I wasn't ready. The taste of my bonded faded, and an immense sadness took their place. We stood in silence for a long moment.

"So, are we leaving?" I asked finally. The guys exchanged guilty expressions of misery that had unease crawling up my spine. "What's going on?"

I turned at the purr of a car engine behind us. Panic bled into me, turning my veins into ice as three black sedans wearing the Institute logo pulled into the parking lot. Dread dropped my stomach to the floor. How did they find us?

It doesn't matter—they're too late. We're bonded now.

I cowered behind Rafe and Ares, digging my fingers into their backs as a beta woman in her late thirties stepped out of the car. She was tall and willowy and wore a crisp white pantsuit, with her hair up in a severe bun. She was everything I wasn't.

"Hi, hon." The lady's voice was sickly sweet. "I'm so happy we found you."

I trembled as I burrowed my face into Rafe's back, taking in deep, sucking breaths, trying to chase what little of his comforting smell I could still find with the blockers working their way through my system. This woman needed to understand I couldn't go with her.

"I'm staying with them," I said into Rafe's shoulder, refusing to meet her eyes. I peeked up at my guys, instead, surprised to see agony rather than resolve. *Why aren't they saying anything?* "Tell her. We're a pack."

Rafe twisted, pushing me out in front of him. Relief filled me. He'd keep me safe and show her that I belonged with them.

His voice was flat as it rumbled against my back. "Thanks for coming. She's ready to go."

Pain pierced through my chest. I couldn't breathe.

I turned, reaching desperately for Ares instead, fingers grasping at his arm. "What's happening?"

He took a step closer to me, and hope lifted my daze, but it froze in my lungs as he stopped just out of my reach. Confusion wrapped around me as I met his dejected eyes.

Nox broke my loose grip on Ares, and I spun to him, fighting his grip. "Nox?"

His expression was a blank wall, closed to me as he nudged me toward the strange woman, his words burning my ears. "They'll be able to take care of you, Little Wolf."

This couldn't be happening. "I don't understand. Why?"

The woman from the Omega Institute nodded, smiling with too much teeth. She seemed to agree with that statement.

I choked on my breath, and hot tears streamed down my face, as the realization of what was happening finally sank in. I met each of their gazes, searching for something familiar, but they might as well have been strangers.

"You said *you* would take care of me," I pleaded as a tremble ran through me.

Ares looked over my shoulder at Rafe. He gave a quick shake of his head, a hint of doubt there.

I turned back to Rafe, offering him a hopeful smile. *Maybe he'll change his mind?*

Rafe crossed his arms, his expression blank. "Yeah, until we realized what that actually means." His tone was harsher than I'd ever heard it. "You're going to get us killed, Bliss. You need to go. Sorry, but we're not about to die for you."

I sucked in a breath, begging for a taste of what they were feeling. I couldn't believe it. It didn't make sense. "But—"

"Make her go," Nox hissed so low I could barely make it out.

Ares growled. "Fuck you."

I met his icy-blue gaze, a sliver of emotion breaking through the wall. I thought I saw regret there, but he'd shut it down too fast to be sure.

Killian stepped into me and dropped his head close to mine. Tears pooled in my eyes as he tucked a piece of hair behind my ear. He scanned my face, lingering for half a second too long. He took a deep breath, and his lips tipped up in the corner, but there was a wrongness to them. "It's going to be okay, baby. It's going to turn out fine."

"No." The world dropped out from under me, and I shook my head at him. My voice cracked around the vowels. "This isn't how it's supposed to be. I...I know you don't want this." I dug my fingers into his shirt and pulled myself into him, refusing to let him go. "Tell them, Kill. Tell them you're my pack."

I reached for my senses. I could've sworn I tasted hurt there, but Killian's face was completely blank. His thumb ran over my jaw one last time as his bark filled the space. "Go with them. Now."

I gasped, and betrayal wrapped around me. My trust in them splintered. They didn't want me. Tears burned my skin as his bark forced me to take a step toward the woman. I had no choice but to follow her into the black sedan. I pushed against my instincts, fighting as they shut the door after me. The click of the locks pierced the air.

The hole in my chest threatened to consume me. The same bonds that moments before had felt like coming home, anchoring themself into every part of me, now left me hollow. Everything I thought was all a lie. Some kind of teenage fantasy of a girl desperate for boys' attention.

I sat, numb in the back of the car, and my heart tore open with every foot that separated us. I watched, hands clenching the seat, as their silhouettes disappeared when the car turned the corner.

The sharply dressed women beside me glanced my way. "It will be okay, Bliss. You'll finally be where you belong."

The echo of her words stung. I *had* a place where I belonged. Or, I thought I did.

Even missing my omega senses, my heart screamed as the newly formed bonds were nearly stretched to their breaking point. The further we drove, the more faint the tug on the tethers between us became. Tears stung my eyes as I fought to hold on to the invisible connection—the only thing I had left to my pack. Distance couldn't sever the bonds, but that didn't stop my soul from feeling their loss.

Killian was the first to fade, his joy slipping away until I almost couldn't feel him at all. Nox's calm understanding went next, followed by Rafe's protection. I gasped and had to choke down a sob as the last bond went dormant, and Ares' unconditional acceptance of me disappeared with it.

I bit my lip to hide its wobble as my heart shredded in my chest. I would never see them again. They'd let me go, knowing we would lose each other forever. Not one of them helped me as I begged them. They knew what they were doing, and none of them moved to keep me. They got rid of their needy little omega. Too much work to keep around. Too much of a burden.

The ache in my chest became unbearable.

Rejected.

That was what they called it when your pack abandoned you and left you to the wolves. Because that's what the Institute was: a bunch of wolves preparing you for your new master.

Pain burned through my chest as I closed each door to my heart, building a wall brick by brick. The bond wouldn't break no matter how many years passed, but I could protect myself from it. I would turn myself to ice and become the perfect little omega, giving the guys exactly what they wanted. The next time they saw me would be on the TV, mated to a new man. Rejecting them right back.

All I'd have to do was survive without them.

Continued in Pack Bound

Available Spring 2022

Pre-Order Now

Want more from the authors?

The Gentlemen Series

Read Now

Need someone to share theories with?

Join Kate King & Jessa Wilder Reader Gang

JOIN NOW

Join Our Facebook Group:
Kate King & Jessa Wilder Reader Gang
TikTok:
https://www.tiktok.com/@kateking_jessawilder?lang=en
Instagram:
https://www.instagram.com/kateking_jessawilder/
Get all the latest news first by signing up to Kate and Jessa's mailing list: https://katekingjessawilder.com
Website: https://katekingjessawilder.com

Printed in Great Britain
by Amazon

75808921R10058